For Captain Nemo

First published 2001
1 3 5 7 9 10 8 6 4 2
© Babette Cole 2001

Babette Cole has asserted her right under
the Copyright, Designs and Patents Act, 1988,
to be identified as the author of this work

First published in the United Kingdom in 2001 by
Jonathan Cape
The Random House Group Limited
20 Vauxhall Bridge Road
London SWlV 2SA

The Random House Group Limited Reg. No. 954009
www.randomhouse.co.uk

A catalogue record of this book
is available from the British Library

ISBN 0 224 04717 5

Printed in Singapore by Tien Wah Press (Pte) Ltd

TRUE LOVE

Babette Cole

A TOM MASCHLER BOOK

JONATHAN CAPE
LONDON

Now they've got that new baby,
they don't want me any more.

Love feels like a warm puppy.

OW!

Love means sharing.

Truelove, no!

Love cures all hurt.

Oh, well.

Love gives you strength.

Truelove!
Put that down!

It makes you notice those you love.

Love makes your heart sing.

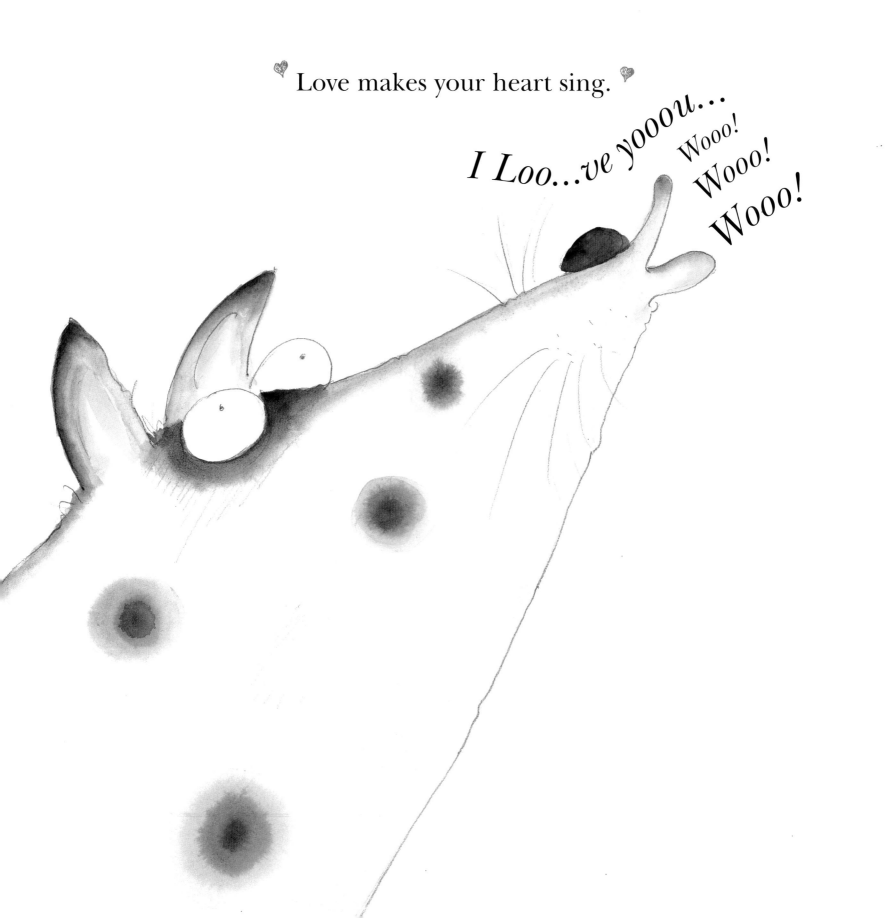

That's it, Truelove. Out!

Love means there's always somewhere
to shelter from the storm.

And like sunshine after rain,
it can lead to a new beginning.

Love means caring for others...

...and being everyone's best friend.

Love makes you do silly things sometimes.

Hey, can anyone drive?

Love sometimes means losing control.

You can never escape from love.

You miss love when it's not there.

Where's Truelove?

Hello, police?

Love is being found when you are lost.

Love means thinking of others.

Of course they can come too.

Love means forgiveness.

We're so sorry, Truelove.

That's OK.

Now I know what love really means.